BEW...
DO NOT...
BOO...
BEGINNING TO END

Whether you know it or not, you're about to take part in a secret mission. You will meet danger and excitement with every twist and turn of the plot. Will you be captured by a terrorist organization and spend the rest of your days working on a prison work farm? Will you be the hero who saves the life of a king and averts World War III? It all depends on the choices you make!

Read each page. Then follow the instructions at the bottom. Weigh your choices carefully. A bad decision could mean danger or even death! Good luck on your mission — this message will self-destruct in 30 seconds!

Start your mission on PAGE 2.

"When I joined the U.S. Junior Track and Field Team, I didn't bargain for a midnight meeting — in a cave," you whisper nervously to your teammate Dale Cooper. "What's happening, anyway?"

"Coach Ward says they may be cancelling our exhibition tour," Dale hisses back, "because it's too dangerous."

You hope he's wrong, but *something* funny is definitely going on. An hour ago you and the 24 other players scheduled to leave for Europe in the morning were sound asleep in your hotel rooms. Now you're assembled in a cavern with stalactites hanging from the ceiling, closed-circuit TV cameras panning the room, and tough-looking Marine guards at the door. And you are one scared and puzzled bunch of kids.

Suddenly, a huge projection screen descends from the roof. A man in a trench coat steps up to the platform facing your chairs. He looks just like Humphrey Bogart, except for one small detail — he has a metal hook instead of a left hand!

"Thank you for coming, and welcome to ACI headquarters," he rasps. "You'll have to pardon the primitive facilities. But we move around a lot."

"What's ACI and who are you, anyway?" someone in your row has the nerve to mumble.

Go on to PAGE 4.

"Glad you asked," the guy shoots back. "For this operation, my code name is Raven. As for ACI, it's the most hush-hush of all the U.S. intelligence agencies. Compared to us, the CIA is a Boy Scout troop."

Before you can react, a huge map of Europe flashes onto the screen behind Raven. Solonia, a small country between Belgium and Luxembourg, glows bright orange.

You nudge Dale. "Hey, that's the first stop on our tour."

His answer is muffled by a whirring noise. To your amazement, Raven's hook begins to grow like Pinocchio's nose. In a few seconds it's long enough to use as a pointer, which he thumps against the map of Solonia.

"This is top secret information, but within the month an international terrorist organization called BRUTE is planning to overthrow King Idle of Solonia.

"You've got to decide whether to proceed as planned, or bypass Solonia, or cancel the entire trip. But before you vote on which course of action to take, let me fill you in on a few facts. If you bypass Solonia, BRUTE will know we're onto their assassination plot. That will make it harder for us to protect the king, and the whole incident could blow up into World War III."

Go on to PAGE 5.

"If you proceed as planned, the entire team may be in danger. I don't want to influence you in any way, but the security of the free world could be riding on your decision. On the other hand, if you decide to take the chickens' way out and not go at all, we can tell the press the trip was cancelled due to lack of funds. The U.S. will be the laughingstock of the International Athletic Commission. But don't let that worry you. It's perfectly all right with us."

Raven's story sounds so fantastic that you can't quite believe it. But there's Coach Ward starting to poll the team members for their vote. When he reaches your seat, he gives you a penetrating look. "I have eight junior spies who want to go to Solonia, eight heartless athletes who don't mind putting King Idle's head on the chopping block, and eight chickens. It's all up to you."

What a position this puts you in! Should you vote to put yourself and 24 other athletes in danger? Should you play it semisafe, or are you afraid to cross the road?

If you decide to bypass Solonia, turn to PAGE 17.

If you decide to go to Solonia, go on to PAGE 6.

If you decide to stay home, you might as well stop reading this book. Didn't you pick it up with adventure in mind? Maybe you should rethink your travel plans.

Is Solonia for real? you wonder 24 hours later, looking around at the Blandsburg airport. This may be the capital city, but the terminal is so small that there's only one gate. The passengers debarking from your plane must wait for a group of departing Chinese acupuncturists to clear customs. While you're stuck in line, a nervous young man in a trench coat and slouch hat approaches the team.

"I'm Hurtz Pullet from the *Blandsburg Morning Evening Globe Mail Express Times Herald Post,*" he announces in a shaky voice that makes you wonder if he's stating a fact or apologizing.

Coach Ward lifts a questioning eyebrow. "You mean you represent *eight* different papers?"

"No," the young man admits. "Just one. There isn't much action here in Solonia, so over the years, the *Globe, Mail, Express, Times,* etc., merged to stay in business. But your visit is really big news. How about some interviews?"

You're all set to be the Solonian media event of the century when the coach bursts your bubble. "I'm sorry," he explains. "But we've been advised to keep a low profile."

Go on to PAGE 7.

"Can't you even tell me why?" Pullet pleads. "I only got this assignment because our star reporter is sick. This was my one chance to make the front page. Besides, I told you nothing ever happens here."

"Aw, that can't be true," Dale challenges.

"Oh, yes it can. What do you expect when King Idle has made marathon sleeping the national sport, the royal flag is gray on gray, and the national anthem only has two notes?"

That does sound pretty boring. And you can't help feeling sorry for the poor reporter as he slouches out of the terminal.

"Hey, Dale," you whisper. "Save my place. I'm going to get a drink of water."

"But Coach Ward told us to stay together," your friend protests.

"I'll only be a minute," you say as you head for the exit. Out in the baggage claim area, you come face to face with Pullet.

"Say, aren't you one of the U.S. Junior Track and Field Team members?" he questions.

With your red, white, and blue jogging suit and flight bag, that's hard to deny.

"Then how about an interview?"

You really want to do it. But what about Coach Ward's reaction and Raven's warning?

If you decide to talk, turn to PAGE 9.
If you turn Pullet down, turn to PAGE 24.

Quickly you get dressed, grab the suspicious bag, and dash up to Coach Ward's room on the 57th floor. You have to knock twice before anyone comes to the door. But when it finally opens, someone yanks you roughly inside. And it's not the coach. It's Raven.

"What, what are you doing here?" you stutter, beginning to realize you may have made a mistake.

"I was waiting to see which team members didn't trust us. Luckily for me, you're the only one who questioned our note."

Somehow his gruff tone and menacing look tell you that lucky for him isn't going to be lucky for you. "BRUTE doesn't like any loose ends," he adds, confirming your worst fears.

"BRUTE," you gasp. "Are you a member of BRUTE?"

"But of course. Why else would I want to compromise the whole American team?"

Maybe you can edge back out the door, you hope. But Raven's bionic hook shoots out and grabs you by the neck. "Unfortunate fall you had," he says, giving you a strong push toward the window.

THE END

"Sure, I'd love to be interviewed by the *Post*," you admit, grinning up at him.

"Then let's sit down," he suggests.

"Where should I start?" you ask. "I've never been interviewed before."

Turn to PAGE 12.

After repeating the code word aloud several times, you hungrily follow instructions. You stick a corner of the note in your mouth. It's raspberry-flavored!

When you get to the lobby, everyone else on the team is carrying a bag just like yours. If you're being fooled, so is everyone else.

"What flavor was your note?" Dale Cooper asks.

"Raspberry."

"Hey, lucky, mine was prune."

A few minutes later, Coach Ward gathers everybody together. "Wait here while I check the luggage," he orders.

You're so tired from your sleepless night that you collapse into a chair and watch as the other team members practice the 50-yard dash in front of the bell captain's desk.

But in the midst of the ruckus, you get a shivery feeling and look around anxiously. Everything seems normal, until you spot a sharp-nosed old lady dressed in black sitting on a sofa reading a magazine. Every few moments she peers up over the top of the magazine at you and the other team members. Beside her is a red, white, and blue bag, just like yours. Something about her makes you so nervous that you stand up and grab your own bag protectively.

Go on to PAGE 11.

A moment later, she gets up, too. Leaning heavily on a cane and clutching her flight bag, she totters across the rug toward you. When she gets close, you sniff the strong scent of gardenias. But you don't have much time to think about it, because her cane catches in a worn place on the carpet. As she pitches forward, her flight bag falls. Instinctively, you drop your own bag and reach out to break her fall. She lands in your arms instead of on her face. *Funny,* you think, *she's awfully heavy for someone who looks so frail.*

"Oh, how clumsy of me," she sputters. "Thank you so much, dearie. I'm just lucky you athletes have such fast reflexes."

"Glad I could help," you reply.

The old woman quickly picks up her flight bag and hobbles off toward the elevator.

It's then that an awful thought strikes you. Maybe she has the wrong bag. Hastily you look inside yours. You find three dull brass keys, a pair of new shoelaces, and 19 short yellow pencils. Hey, wait a minute — weren't there only 18 pencils? Or did you count wrong the first time?

If you think you have the right bag, turn to PAGE 13.

If you think the old lady switched bags on you, turn to PAGE 92.

"Uh, this is my first time, too. Just tell me whatever you want, and I'll try to get it all down."

"Okay," you agree. "Well, I was born . . ."

A half hour later, you've told him about your first step, your first loose tooth, your first-grade teacher. You don't notice Pullet has dozed off at your side. But then his snoring gets so loud that even you can't hear what you're saying. Just as you're about to wake him up, you feel the coldness of metal on your arm. Oh, no! It's Raven's hook. And he's not too pleased.

"Just making friends with the natives," you explain nervously.

"Disobeying orders could be a deadly offense," he barks as he drags you away.

In a secluded corner, he lets you have it. "Kid, you've really blown it. This is an unforgivable breach of security. You're going home on the next plane."

You feel awful! You didn't mean to breach security. You just wanted to be famous.

"Please, give me another chance," you choke out. "Why don't we flip a coin? If it's heads, you let me stay. If it's tails, you can send me home."

"Okay, gambling is my weak spot," Raven relents.

Flip a coin.
If it's heads, turn to PAGE 20.
If it's tails, turn to PAGE 16.

I must have counted those pencils wrong the first time, you tell yourself as you zip up the bag. Just then a Budget Charter Bus pulls up at the hotel door.

"Okay, everybody outside," Coach Ward calls. You're so excited that you leave the flight bag on the chair. The bus is ready to pull away when you remember.

"Hey, wait," you shout, jumping out of your seat and heading back to the hotel. "I forgot my bag."

You're just about to step into the lobby when a terrible explosion inside knocks you flat on the marble steps. The last thing you remember is the smell of gardenias. When you regain consciousness, you're on a stretcher being taken to the hospital. Beside you are Dale and Coach Ward.

"You saved our lives by leaving that flight bag inside," your friend explains.

"I don't know how BRUTE did it, but there was a pencil bomb inside," says Coach Ward.

"Too bad you're going to miss the trip. But I'll send you postcards from every city," Dale consoles you as they load you into the ambulance.

Even though you lose your place on the team, a major TV network features your bedside commentary when they highlight the trip on the evening news.

THE END

"Fasten your seat belts — we'll be landing in Solonia shortly," the captain advises. "We've made arrangements for ground transportation to complete your travel arrangements."

Waiting for you at Solonia International Airport are two old vans. The other members of the team pack into the first one. You and Dale end up in the second — along with a caged German shepherd who wags his tail and tries to lick you through the wire mesh. The first van pulls quickly ahead, and soon you lose sight of it. But there's plenty to see on the drive through the rolling Solonian countryside with its neat farms and storybook villages. The road, however, isn't in the best condition and neither are the van's shocks. Every time it hits a bump, you wonder if it's going to fall apart.

The scenery changes abruptly as the road swings into a deep forest. You bump along past trees and more trees for over an hour, when the rickety van finally lurches to a halt.

The driver starts mumbling to himself in Solonian. Then he pulls a book out of the glove compartment and begins to thumb hurriedly through the pages. Suddenly he throws the book on the floor, jumps out of the bus, and rushes off into the woods. Soon he's lost from view.

Go on to PAGE 15.

You and Dale look at each other in horror. What are you going to do? Should you stay with the bus and hope somebody comes along this deserted stretch to rescue you? Or should you go for help? And what about the dog?

If you stay in the bus, turn to PAGE 18.

If you leave the dog in the bus and go for help with Dale, turn to PAGE 25.

If you and Dale take the dog along with you and go for help, turn to PAGE 19.

Tough luck! The coin you toss comes up tails. Before you can ask for the best two out of three, Raven puts you on the next flight home. When you get there, your picture is plastered all over the local paper. It seems ACI has fed the wire services a phony cover story. Everybody thinks you tripped in the airport and sprained your ankle. You're the laughingstock of the track circuit. But as the only member of the U.S. Junior Track and Field Team to make the papers, you're now a household word — in Solonia and back home, too. The publicity is good for $20,000 worth of endorsements from Wozo Crunch, the first sugar cereal that boasts that it's really oat-flavored breakfast candy.

THE END

Is skipping Solonia really the right decision? you wonder as you toss and turn all night. The next morning you're so tired you can hardly force yourself to get out of bed. But your eyes snap open when you discover a new red, white, and blue flight bag on the edge of the bathtub. Cautiously you unzip it to discover a pair of new shoelaces, three dull brass keys, 18 short yellow pencils, and a note that says:

This bag and the code word "mustang" will be your passport to freedom if you get captured by BRUTE. Keep the bag with you at all times. After memorizing the code word, swallow this note.

The only signature is a black bird in the corner.

It must be from Raven. But is it on the level, or is someone playing a trick? Should you really swallow the note, or should you take it and the flight bag to Coach Ward?

If you decide to tell Coach Ward, turn to PAGE 8.

If you follow Raven's instructions, turn to PAGE 10.

"If we just sit here in the bus, there ought to be a car along sooner or later," Dale reasons.

"Yeah," you agree. But after two hours of sitting, you're not so sure.

"Gee, I feel like my hands and feet are falling asleep," you tell your friend.

"Me, too," he agrees.

"Even Shep over there hasn't moved in a half hour," you point out. "If I didn't know better, I'd think he'd turned to stone."

With an effort, Dale reaches over to pet the dog. "Oh, my gosh!" he screams. "He *has* turned to stone."

Suddenly your chest tightens with panic. You'd like to run, but your body won't obey.

With every ounce of will you can muster, you lean forward to look at the book the driver threw on the floor. It's fallen open to a page that says:

"The beautiful region of Solonia known as the petrified forest has inspired awe and terror for centuries. Legend has it that during the confluence of certain planets — principally Mars, Pluto, and Jupiter — in their celestial houses, any man or beast trapped in the forest turns to stone."

You glance over at Dale. He's trying to move his stony lips. And with a tremendous effort he finally gets out the words

THE END

The shepherd barks joyfully as you let him out of his cage.

"Good boy," you murmur, patting his head encouragingly. "Can you lead us to safety?"

"*Urf, urf,*" he answers, pawing at the door of the van.

As soon as you release the door, the dog races off down the road — with you and Dale jogging behind. But when he turns off into the woods, you and Dale stop short. Does this dog know where he's going? As if to answer your question, the shepherd circles back and *urfs* encouragingly before dashing off again. Even though you're a long-distance runner, it's hard to keep up with him now. And when Dale gets a stitch in his side, he falls behind.

A few minutes later, you and the dog reach a clearing. Up ahead is a low, concrete building with a sign over the door that reads, ACI/SOLONIAN SUBSTATION.

Rushing toward the door, you grab the handle. "Don't go in there!" Dale shouts as he emerges from the woods. "It might be a trick."

Should you open the door? Or wait for Dale?

If you decide to open the door, turn to PAGE 26.

If you wait for Dale, turn to PAGE 23.

You're so nervous when you flip the coin that it flies across the pavement and lands under the bench where Pullet is snoring.

"Want me to crawl under and get it?" you ask.

Raven shakes his head. "I'll give you the benefit of the doubt, since the next flight home doesn't depart for a week, anyway."

By now the team has already left for a guided tour of the city. So Raven takes you to your hotel to wait for them. But the room doesn't even have a TV. What can you do for amusement, you wonder, rummaging through the old bureau next to the bed. In the top drawer is a tattered English/Solonian map of Blandsburg. Luckily, the back has a list of the major points of interest — all five of them. Four are on the other side of town. But the Historical Museum is only a few blocks away. Maybe you can spend the afternoon there.

Out on the street, you study the map to get your bearings. (Study the map on page 21 and keep reading.)

There seem to be two routes to the museum. Military Road cuts across the park. But Burger Avenue runs through the business district. Which should you take?

If you decide to stroll through the park, turn to PAGE 36.

If you decide to walk through the business district, turn to PAGE 59.

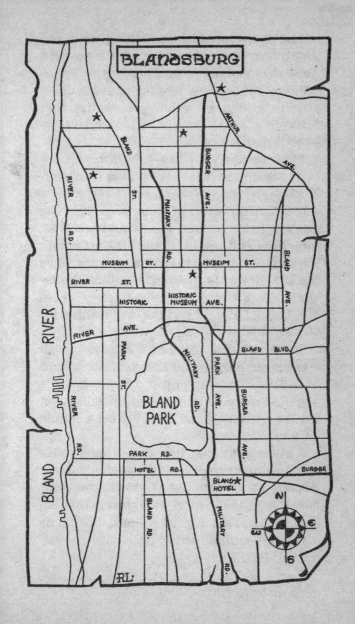

Just then you feel something cold and sharp on your shoulder. Afraid to turn around, you hear a familiar, raspy voice, "You're going to be late for your plane."

With a sigh of relief, you realize that Raven's got you hooked. Quickly you explain what happened.

"Let me see your bag," he directs.

You watch as he checks it over carefully.

"False alarm," he reports. "Everything's okay." After giving back your bag, he reaches in his pocket, whips out his wallet, and flips it open like *Star Trek*'s Captain Kirk snapping open his communicator. "I've found our wayward team member," he reports. "We'll be down momentarily." Five minutes later you're on the bus heading for the airport.

An hour later you and the team are on a jumbo jet heading for Europe. Coach Ward is kept busy running up and down the aisle handing out peanut butter sandwiches. But you're so excited you can only eat a couple of bites.

This is your first trip abroad, and nothing's going to spoil it — not even when the captain announces that a terrorist group has taken over the airport at your destination. You think it's a big joke, until the plane does a 90-degree turn.

Turn to PAGE 14.

Dale is probably right. Charging blindly into a strange building in the woods might not be so smart.

"Let's hear your idea," you suggest.

"Send the dog in first!"

"Good thinking," you agree and then turn to the dog. "Okay, boy. Check it out."

He licks your hand, wags his tail one more time, and bounds off down the long passage on the other side of the door. But before he gets very far, the floor drops out from under him, and you hear an anguished *awwwooo* . . . as he vanishes.

You and Dale look at each other and shudder. Poor Shep. You wouldn't have sent him in there if you'd known that was going to happen. "Maybe we ought to try and find our way back to the bus, after all," you suggest in a very quiet voice.

The two of you turn and start back down the trail. But without the dog, finding your way through the woods is a bit more confusing.

Two hours later you're hopelessly lost, and it's getting dark and cold. What's more, it's been hours since you ate that half a peanut butter sandwich back on the airplane.

Turn to PAGE 28.

Pullet's offer of instant fame is tempting. But you just can't go against instructions.

"Sorry," you explain. "You heard my coach."

There's a look on Pullet's face that you can't quite read. "I was hoping you hadn't heard him," he admits. "But at least let me give you a souvenir of Solonia." Reaching under his slouch hat, he pulls out a shiny gray button. Written across the front, in fancy black letters, are the words, SOLONIA IS FOR SURPRISES!

"I'll pin it on you," the reporter offers.

Turn to PAGE 30.

"Should we stick to the road or try to find our way through the woods?" you ask Dale.

"Aw, come on, where's your sense of adventure?" he challenges, stepping off the blacktop and into the thick forest. "I learned all about finding my way through the woods at Camp Gitchamagoomi."

Two hours later, you're so lost you can't even find your sense of adventure.

"That's the last time I'll listen to your advice," you inform Dale.

He shakes his head. "This never happened at camp. The trees in Solonia must be different or something."

"Yeah!" you agree, sitting down on a fallen log in a little clearing. It's getting dark and cold. And from the growling in your stomach, you know it's way past dinner time.

As the shadows lengthen, you hear spooky rustlings in the underbrush. And when an acorn falls from a nearby tree, you and Dale both jump up as if someone had fired a rifle shot.

"I'm scared," your friend confesses. "Let's sit with our backs to each other, so we can keep guard in both directions."

That seems like a good idea.

Turn to PAGE 28.

You open the door cautiously and step into pitch blackness.

Before you can back out again, a strong hand grabs the back of your neck and another slaps a wet cloth over your face. The last thing you remember is the overpowering smell of gardenias.

When you wake up, you're lying in a pile of straw on a hard stone floor. *Where am I?* you wonder, too groggy to sit up. Your head hurts so much, it's hard to think. So you just lie there with your eyes closed. And lucky for you.

"Still unconscious," you hear a man's deep voice snort. "The drug worked like a charm. I knew they wouldn't have time to give all those kids the antidote before they left the hotel. And no one will think to look for the missing team member here in the dungeon under King Idle's castle."

KING IDLE?! He's the king of Solonia! The man with the deep voice goes on and confirms your worst suspicions: "As soon as our little puppet wakes up, we'll pull the strings to put our assassination plot into action!"

Go on to PAGE 27.

"Not so fast," a woman's voice warns. "Remember our instructions. We must administer the test first. We'll give our athlete an almost impossible mental task — answering all our questions in rhyme. If the drug worked, the rhymes will come easily. If not, we'll just kill the little creep."

You realize the creep is you!

You hear a heavy metal door clang shut and two sets of footsteps retreating.

Oh, no! You shudder. These BRUTE agents have you under their control. Or have they? Could the raspberry-flavored note you swallowed back at the hotel have been the antidote? Maybe there's a way to find out.

Since they want you to answer questions with a rhyme, you'll try it and see what happens. "What are my favorite foods?" you ask yourself. "Pickle brickle, ready spaghetti, and any sweet treat." A shiver goes up your spine and your palms start to sweat as you realize what you've said. Either you *are* under BRUTE's control, or you're a lot smarter than you thought. But before you have any more time to wonder about it, you hear a key turning in the lock of the heavy metal door across the dungeon.

Does BRUTE have you under control? If you think so, turn to PAGE 84.

If you think you still have free will but can fool your captors, turn to PAGE 34.

The two of you are peering anxiously into the gathering gloom when the faint sounds of fiddle music reach your ears.

"Am I crazy," you whisper to Dale, "or is somebody playing 'Turkey in the Straw'?"

"I hear it, too," he confirms. "Maybe where there's 'Turkey in the Straw,' there's something to eat."

The two of you start off in the direction of the music. But it's tough going in the dark through the tangled underbrush. After what seems like miles, you see the flicker of campfires ahead. And you can hear the sounds of people talking and laughing.

As you get closer, you see what looks like five plush motor homes drawn into a circle around several campfires. But the people inside the circle don't look like typical campers. The women are all wearing long, brightly colored dresses decorated with lots of spangles. And the men have baggy white shirts, red sashes at the waist, and loose-fitting black pants. They must be gypsies — traveling in style.

In jogging suits, you and Dale will stick out like sore thumbs. While you're trying to figure out what to do, the decision is made for you. Suddenly you feel a large hand clamp your shoulder.

"Good eevening," a gruff voice intones. "What can wee do to — uh, for — you?"

Turn to PAGE 35.

I'm sorry," you tell Pullet. "I don't think Coach Ward would want me to accept any gifts."

Pullet is obviously thrown by your refusal. He's so flustered that he drops his pad and pencil. And when he leans over to pick them up, his hat falls off, too. The only way he can catch his balance is to grab your waist. The whole thing reminds you of a pickpocket routine you saw on a TV situation comedy last week. But you know you don't have anything worth stealing, so you're not worried.

"Sorry," Pullet apologizes. "It's an old Ping-Pong injury that acts up at the strangest times."

"Oh, that's okay," you assure him as you head back to claim your place in line.

Turn to PAGE 47.

Although no one speaks to you, everyone keeps stealing glances at you from under hooded lids. And you shiver as the formerly happy fiddle music turns to a minor key. The sound reminds you of a funeral. Even though your stomach is full, you wonder if you'd be better off in the woods. But when you try to stand up, your legs won't support you. And you're suddenly so groggy that you can't keep your eyes open.

"Well, I guess we've taken care of those ACI spies," you hear someone chuckle in the background.

"Gee, I hope they didn't poison the stew," Dale chokes out. You try to answer. But of course you can't because this is

THE END

You agree with Dale. The stew is so horrible that you dump it in the fire when nobody's looking. *Maybe we'd be better off in the woods, after all,* you think.

Dale must be on the same wavelength, because he suddenly stands up and announces to no one in particular, "Well, uh, thanks for the dinner."

"Oh, we wouldn't theenk of letting you go," the man who found you disagrees, as he steps forward into the firelight. "The wolves are very hungry thees time of the year, you know."

Before you can protest, he shoves you and Dale into one of their tents, throws a couple of old blankets in behind you, and pulls the flaps closed. At first you can hear noise and talking all around. But after the violin plays taps, the camp turns ghostly quiet — except for the occasional howl of a wolf in the distance.

Shuddering, you pull the wool cover up around your shoulders. You're still wide-awake when the sound of hushed whispers drifts your way. At first you wish they'd go away and let you sleep. But then you hear a squeaky little voice plead, "Tell me again how to read that message I intercepted when I shot down the ACI carrier pigeon." Your ears tune into the conversation like an antenna tracking a satellite.

Go on to PAGE 33.

"Listen, Boris, if I've told you once, I've told you a thousand times, any BRUTE agent worth his salt has to be able to read ACI communications, not just intercept their birds."

"Did you hear that?" Dale whispers. "It sounds like these guys are BRUTE agents."

"*Shhh*," you hiss. "If they know we're listening, we could be in real trouble."

Turn to PAGE 56.

Shakily you sit up and open your eyes. "Glad to see you're awake," the woman you heard before snaps. She's tall and thin, has stringy black hair, and is wearing a maid's uniform. The man with her, who is at least a foot shorter and 50 pounds heavier, is dressed like a stable hand.

"All right," the maid continues, getting right down to business, "who should swim south for the winter?"

Desperately, you try to think as she begins to tap her foot impatiently. "A pale whale!" you finally gasp.

The odd couple exchange satisfied looks. "Very good. And what do you get when your lemon pie explodes?"

"A, ur, a meringue bang?" you sputter.

"Not bad," the tubby stable hand congratulates you. "Let's try one more to see how sharp you are. Where do you go to school?"

Your mind goes blank.

"I told you this would never work. We should have gotten rid of our little guest right away," the maid snaps.

Desperately you try to think of a rhyming answer.

Can you come up with something fast? You've only got a minute. Try it and see.

If you think of an appropriate rhyme, go to PAGE 37.

If you can't, turn to PAGE 86.

You're almost too terrified to speak. But as the fingers on your shoulder tighten, you force yourself to answer. "We, we're lost."

"And hungry," Dale chips in.

"Come!" your captor grunts, pushing you toward the circle of campers. In the flickering light, someone shoves a metal plate full of hot stew into your hand.

"Ugh!" Dale whispers after one bite." This tastes worse than the stuff from the school cafeteria." You agree. But should you eat it anyway?

If you do, turn to PAGE 31.
If you don't, turn to PAGE 32.

You tuck the map in your pocket and head for the park, where expanses of green lawns and carefully trimmed hedges stretch in every direction.

It's so peaceful that you can't hear anything but birds chirping — and something else — the sound of stealthy footsteps on the walk behind you. Every time you stop, they stop. But each time you whirl around, there's nothing to see except a bush quivering right beside the path. Are you really being followed by a bush?

This can't be happening, you shudder, quickening your pace. Why would anyone be following little old you? And then your mind flashes back to that midnight meeting with Raven before you left for Solonia. He warned you about BRUTE — the international terrorist organization out to assassinate the king. And he was worried they might try to drag the track team into the middle of their devious plot.

Just ahead is the imposing stone front of the museum. It's a brooding medieval fortress with turrets at every corner. If you go inside, maybe you'll never get out again. On the other hand, it might be the only safe place around.

If you decide to go into the museum, turn to PAGE 40.

If you decide to make a run for it, turn to PAGE 38.

Your captors repeat the question. "Where do you go to school?"

"An elementary penitentiary," you say. It's not great, but they don't seem to care. You've fooled them! "We'll be back for you later," the stable hand growls. Since he's sure you're in his power, he doesn't even bother to lock the door.

Now's the time to escape, you think to yourself.

For the first time you have a chance to examine your cell. You look around. The manacles on the wall and the torture rack in the corner give you the shivers. And the air smells as if it's been bottled up for a good 200 years.

Is there any way to sneak out of this place? you wonder, looking upward. There's a ventilator grate in the ceiling, but it's too high to reach. However, as you continue your search, you also find a trapdoor under the straw you're lying on. And across the room from the unlocked door is a dark opening in the brick wall. Maybe it's the beginning of a tunnel.

Turn to PAGE 39.

Glancing over your shoulder, you see that the ever-present bush is now only 10 feet from where you're standing. You've got to get away, and fast.

Quickly you sprint around the back of the museum — where you find yourself facing an eight-lane avenue. The only cross street is way down the block, but the pedestrian light nearby is still green. Just as your foot touches the curb, however, the signal turns yellow. You come to a screeching halt — and feel the scratch of branches against your neck. Should you dash across and pray you can beat the traffic, or should you try to make it back around to the front of the museum again?

If you decide to have another go at the museum entrance, turn to PAGE 40.

If you decide to cross the street, turn to PAGE 58.

Suddenly the idea of staying in this filthy cell any longer gives you the creeps. So you use all your knowledge and intuition to pick the most likely escape route.

If you think you should make a break through the door your captors left un- locked, turn to PAGE 87.

If you think you should try the trapdoor under the straw, turn to PAGE 43.

If you think your chances are best with the dark opening in the wall, turn to PAGE 45.

You decide your only option is the museum. Without looking back you take the museum's marble steps two at a time, throw yourself through the door, and crash into the ticket booth. As you pick yourself up, you bump your head on a sign written in 13 languages. The English line informs you: *ADMISSION 500 DURKAS.*

You don't even know what a durka is, much less have 500 of them. But when the door bangs in the wind and some leaves blow inside, you frantically start reading the fine print. It reads: MAJOR CHARGE CARDS ACCEPTED.

Thank goodness you didn't leave home without your National Express Card.

Inside, the museum turns out to offer a fascinating look at Solonian history. In the main gallery is the horsehair bed where King Idle the First spent most of his reign; the Royal Solonian Crown Jewels, which look like wax-covered grapes; and a giant-size suit of armor that some English knight named Sir Sitwell wore to the Crusades (too bad he only got as far as Solonia). *Gosh, was he a big guy,* you think, looking up at seven feet of beat-up metal.

Go on to PAGE 41.

You stand on tiptoes to get a better look. When you gently tap the shoulder blades of the armor, the rear end opens like the flap in the back of a pair of long johns.

Oh no, I've done it again, you think, as you give the flap a forceful slam shut. Maybe you ought to get out of here before they arrest you for destroying the national treasures.

Hurrying back around the bulky armor, you trip over a red, white, and blue flight bag. It looks just like yours. But you didn't bring it, did you? Could someone else from the team be in the museum? If so, they'll want their bag back.

You've picked up the strap when you hear several sets of heavy footsteps. They don't sound like anybody on your team. Maybe this is a trap.

If you think you should hide, go on to PAGE 42.

If you think you should try to act just like any normal tourist visiting the museum, turn to PAGE 44.

The suit of armor looks like the only place to hide. But when you thump the shoulder this time, the trapdoor in the back doesn't budge. Frantically you rummage inside the bag for something to pry it open. Your hand closes on a metal key. To your surprise and relief it fits into the slot in the rusty armor.

Quickly you dive through the trapdoor. You hear it slam closed behind you about the same time you hit the bottom. "Forsooth! Why hast thou invaded my dwelling?" a thin voice rises up from the toes.

"What?" you whisper.

"If one must pass another 700 years thus, let it be with congenial company."

"Huh? I can't see a thing. Who am I talking to?"

"Sir Sitwell. Who would you suppose?"

"But you've been dead since the Crusades," you gasp.

"Not true. A sorcerer's curse turned my armor into a prison and shrunk me down to the size of your toenail." His voice seems as if it's getting closer. And when you come face to face with him, you realize that you've *shrunk, too!*

"Do you play Fish?" he questions. "I've fashioned quite a serviceable set of cards from chewing gum wrappers visitors have thrown in here. And we've all the time in the world for an extended game."

THE END

The rusted door under your straw is hard to open. But you give a determined yank on a large metal ring, and the door yields with a groan.

The narrow, dark passageway you've uncovered certainly doesn't look very inviting. You force yourself to crawl inside. The rough stone is wet under your hands and knees. And the air smells even mustier than in your cell. As you grope your way along the tunnel, you wonder if you've made a bad mistake. But soon you feel the path sloping upward. You begin to quicken your pace and are heartened when you see a dim light up ahead. The source of the light turns out to be a grate in the floor at the end of the tunnel. However, when you look down the grate, you are devastated to discover you are staring into the same rotten cell. Could you stay here and hide? you wonder. Then you notice the trapdoor you left open. A dead giveaway! You'd better get back to your pile of straw before someone finds out you're missing. You struggle with the floor grate, but it won't budge. There's no room to turn around, so you sigh and start edging your way backward to where you came from. After what seems like hours, you're finally sprawled exhausted on the straw. You'd like nothing better than to go to sleep, but you force yourself to sit up and think.

Turn to PAGE 39.

Grabbing the flight bag, you saunter over to the next exhibit — a display of famous Solonian landscapes. Letting the bag slip noiselessly to the floor, you study the oil paintings on the wall in front of you. Your skin starts to crawl as two military officers walk up and stand on either side of you. They seem to be studying the art with the same intensity as you. But something about them — probably their pistols and over-sized nightsticks — gives you the jitters. The silence is driving you crazy. You've got to move on, and quickly. Casually picking up the bag again, you edge slowly backward. The officers haven't blinked an eye. But just as you're turning, both men spin around and grab your arms in an unbreakable hold.

Turn to PAGE 49.

The hole in the wall of your cell leads to a long tunnel under the castle moat. Soon you're at the other end, peeking out from a huge drainpipe at a bustling marketplace. *What now?* you wonder, dusting off your clothes and looking at the crowds of shoppers. You may be out of King Idle's castle, but you still can't tell the good guys from the bad, and you can't speak Solonian.

The market is crowded with stalls and pushcarts. On all sides, Solonians are haggling enthusiastically with the merchants. But it's all Greek to you. Several stands sell newspapers and magazines. And you can't believe your eyes when you see your picture on the front page of today's paper under a bold black headline. Boy, do you wish you could read Solonian.

It's then that you notice a vendor selling old books. And right on top of a pile is a worn Solonian/English dictionary. What luck!

"How much?" you ask, but the old man behind the counter just nods blankly.

So you point to the book and then take off your watch and offer it to him. That he understands. Faster than you can blink, he's the proud owner of a new super-deluxe digital timepiece with a musical alarm that plays "The Yellow Rose of Texas." And you've got the book.

Go on to PAGE 46.

You duck into a sheltered alcove near the market dumpster to study your dictionary. While you're wondering how to get a free copy of the newspaper, two Solonian shop boys carelessly toss a barrel of trash in the general direction of the dumpster. The bad news is that most of it lands on you. The good news is there's a folded copy of today's paper in the muck.

After brushing wilted lettuce from the dictionary, you start trying to translate the headline. It says: *Porfootune Moltugh Skytinge Garplotbork.* The first three words are straightforward enough. They mean "Authorities looking for missing." But that last one is really tough. Would you believe *Garplotbork* has two meanings — "kidnap victim" and "spy." It all depends on the accent marks — which are too blurred by Worcestershire sauce to read.

What a dilemma! You'd like nothing better than to get some help from the Porfootune. But if they think you're a spy, it's going to be awfully dangerous to turn yourself in.

However, there's no more time to think. A policeman has just turned into the alley where you're hiding and is heading in your direction.

If you decide to get his attention, turn to PAGE 48.

If you're afraid that he'll think you're a spy, turn to PAGE 54.

By the time you get back, Dale has already gone through customs, and you have to go to the end of the line. You can see that nobody's luggage is being searched too carefully — until they get to yours. They dump all your personal belongings onto the table and start ripping out the lining of your flight bag. Although you don't want anyone to know the search is making you nervous, you can't stop your knees from banging together like a pair of castanets.

"That pin's got to be here somewhere," one customs official tells the other. "Maybe we should go on to the body search."

You know what body they're talking about, and you look around frantically for help. But the rest of the team has already gone. Your heart is really in your throat now. And even though you know you haven't done anything wrong, you can't help wanting to run. Should you make a break for it or stay and let them finish their search?

If you decide to run, turn to PAGE 67.
If you decide to stick it out, turn to PAGE 69.

Surrendering to this policeman is more difficult than you might have imagined.

"Help!" you shout.

But he just smiles blandly and shakes his head. Quickly you thumb through the dictionary until you find *help* in Solonian. "Zurk!" you try again. But your pronunciation must be off.

Desperate, you begin to act out your predicament. And as you put your hands over your head and wiggle around, a look of comprehension finally crosses his broad features.

"Cornt ak Um," he says, motioning with his arm for you to follow. A few minutes later you find yourself standing in front of a public restroom.

Thinking he's fulfilled his mission, the policeman turns to leave. You're about to chase him down the street, when a red, white, and blue tour bus swings around the corner.

It's your team, making a pit stop. And are you glad to see them!

"Hey, where have you been?" Dale wants to know. "We thought you were Garplotbork."

"Do you mean a spy or a kidnap victim?" you demand.

Dale shrugs. "What does it really matter in

THE END

"Over here," one soldier growls. You're thrilled he speaks English, but your mood changes when he says, "Let's go, spy!"

"What do you mean? I'm no spy," you choke out. But they don't listen. Before you know it, they're marching you down a hall.

The three of you stop in front of an imposing oak door, with a sign in 13 different languages. The English line proclaims: MINISTER OF CULTURE. Roughly, they push you inside, and you find yourself staring across a Ping-Pong-table-size desk at a short, bald man with beady, black eyes.

"Here's the spy you ordered, Your Graciousness," one officer announces shoving you forward.

Thumping you on the shoulder, one of the guards growls, "Tell the minister what you have to say for yourself."

"Ahhh . . . ah, I ah, don't know," you stammer.

"Nevertheless, we will get to the bottom of this," the guard assures you. "Shall we see what's inside the flight bag?"

Beady Eyes nods quickly. The short guard dumps the contents of the red, white, and blue bag on the broad desk. Yellow pencils, a pair of shoelaces, and some dull brass keys scatter in all directions. But it's the small button that reads, SOLÓNIA IS FOR SURPRISES! that really interests the trio.

Go on to PAGE 50.

"Ahh," the minister breathes, fishing it out and holding it aloft. "Ah ha!"

"That's not even my button! I'm not a spy!" you protest.

"Silence, fool," the guard snaps. 10 minutes later, you're tossed into a musty detention cell. There's nothing to do but stare at the graffiti scrawled on the gray walls. Unfortunately, you can't read a word of it because it's all in Solonian. Hours later, you hear a key turn in the lock, and the door creaks open.

"Me lawyer you," a rotund, middle-aged man announces.

"Oh, great!" you groan. But he doesn't seem to notice your lack of enthusiasm. Instead he rummages in his briefcase and pulls out a Solonian/English dictionary.

"Me hab one deeeel for you," he proclaims, and then begins to frantically flip through the pages of the dictionary.

As you may guess, this turns out to be a rather long and difficult conversation.

Go on to PAGE 51.

SUMMARY OF CONVERSATION:

You have two choices:

1. You can go to the Solonian detention farm until the Minister of Culture has evaluated your case.

2. You can admit your guilt now and be put on public trial.

It takes three more hours of broken interchange to convince you that these are the only alternatives.

If you pick choice #1, go on to PAGE 52.
If you pick choice #2, keep reading on this page.

At least justice in Solonia is speedy. Three hours later you're standing in front of a gray-robed judge. "Plead Snikgack," your lawyer whispers urgently, and there's nothing to do but take his advice.

Turn to PAGE 55.

As soon as you agree to go to the Solonian detention farm, two soldiers hustle you and your flight bag out a side door of the museum. Waiting at the curb is a dilapidated hay cart driven by an ugly little man who reminds you of Rumpelstiltskin.

Quicker than you can say Rumpelstiltskin, you're being pushed into the cart, chained to an iron ring, and covered with loose straw. You hear the guards muttering and cursing you.

You can't see a thing; you itch all over; and the hay is tickling your nose. Suddenly you feel a sneeze coming on. You certainly don't want to draw any attention to yourself right now. If you can hold your breath for 30 seconds, maybe that will stifle the sneeze.

Try it and see.

If you last that long, turn to PAGE 62.
If you can't, turn to PAGE 57.

The only place to hide from the policeman is under the trash. But it's already too late. Just as you're burrowing in, a burly hand grabs your shoulder and pulls you out.

The newspaper you were clutching falls open at your feet. And you see the policeman look incredulously from the picture on the front page to your face and back again.

"Garplotbork!" he growls. Before you know it, you're in a detention cell at the local police station.

But at least there's not a backlog of court cases in Solonia. 45 minutes later you're at the marble-and-gold Palace of Justice, standing in front of a gray-robed judge.

He begins to deliver what you assume is a lecture on the evils of Garplotbork. But you give up trying to translate it after a few words.

Just as you're about to doze off standing up, your lawyer walks in. And to your surprise, it's Raven.

"Plead Snikgack," he whispers urgently. And there's nothing to do but take his advice.

Go on to PAGE 55.

Unfortunately, when you have a chance to look it up, you find that *Snikgack* means "guilty as charged."

"Don't worry," a new lawyer assures you just before they lead you back to your cell. "We have it all arranged. Next week, you're going to be traded for the crew of a Solonian tuna trawler and a second-round draft choice to be determined later."

It turns out to be the longest week of your life. The public address system plays the two-note Solonian national anthem endlessly. And you don't have the stamina to stick your fingers in your ears because all they'll feed you is mashed rutabaga and water. Although you lose 10 pounds, everything works out as promised. You're released right on schedule — so, at least this isn't really

THE END

"Okay, Boris, let's take it from the top. First, turn on your flashlight. Then be sure you have a pencil and paper. On line one of your paper, write the 26 letters of the alphabet across the page. Are you following me so far?"

"Yeah. It's the next part that always stumps me."

"Okay. Well, let's go through it step by step. The ACI code key today is the word GOAT. So on line two, write G-O-A-T under the A-B-C-D. Then write the rest of the alphabet in order under the remaining 22 letters, starting under E. But be sure to leave out G, O, A, and T because you've already used them."

"I think I've got that."

"Take each letter in your coded message, and look for it on line two of the paper you just prepared."

"Hey, the message starts with S, and I've found it!"

"Good. Now what letter is above the S?"

"The T."

"Well, T is the decoded first letter of your message. You can get the rest of the message the same way by substituting each coded letter for the uncoded one above it."

Do you understand the code system? If you do, turn to PAGE 90.

If you don't, read this page again or turn to PAGE 91 for help.

Breath-holding was never your strong suit. "*Ahchooooo!*" You gasp and then stiffen as you hear the wagon screech to a halt.

"Gadgeback!" the officer yells, and points his gun at you. You don't know what *Gadgeback* means, but from the sound of it you don't want to know!

Turn to PAGE 62.

Since you're a world-class sprinter, you start across the street, even though you can hear the engines of the cars and buses revving up.

You've made it across five lanes, when suddenly a blinding pain hits your left calf muscle. It's a cramp. You can hardly walk, much less run. But you have to keep limping along because a bus is bearing down on you.

Suddenly, Officer Safety's first-grade lecture echoes in your mind: "And remember, *never cross against the light!*"

On the bus's bumper is a red sticker with black letters. As it gets closer and closer, the words come into focus. *Oh, no,* you shudder, *Officer Safety was right.* The bumper sticker says

THE END

When you get to the Blandsburg business district, you're enticed by the tantalizing smell of chocolate. Following your nose, you find yourself standing in front of a candy kitchen.

"Do you give out samples?" you ask the gray-haired proprietor hopefully.

"Bot uf course," she answers.

The heck with the museum. You head back to the hotel and devote the rest of the afternoon to crunching away on a five-pound case of chocolate-covered peanut brittle.

Unfortunately, your stomach isn't up to this kind of abuse. And when Coach Ward comes in to find out why you missed supper, you're afraid to tell him. So he calls in the hotel physician. Just your luck, old Doctor Padakia's English is nonexistent. When Coach Ward leaves you alone to be examined, your confidential explanations about eating a case of peanut brittle are misinterpreted.

Dr. Padakia tells Coach Ward that you have a case of "apeanutcitis" and must be operated on immediately in the Royal Solonian Hospital. He's really excited about the prospect, because he hasn't had a chance to perform abdominal surgery in 20 years. Take our word for it, you don't want to hear any gory details. We'll just say this is

THE END

A tall, commanding-looking guard steps forward. "I'll take charge here," he rasps. The voice sounds familiar. And then you feel a metal hook on your sleeve.

"Lucky I was on duty," Raven says, leading you away. "What did you and Porky uncover at the detention farm?" Quickly you fill him in.

"Yes, we suspected the minister. But we must get that microdot for proof," Raven tells you.

The two of you rush to the palace communications center, where Raven makes a tense call to another ACI agent. When he finishes, he turns to you.

"Barney will be glad to wrap this case up. We've had him undercover, disguised as a bush, for the past three months. You don't know how many robins' eggs he's been godfather to."

20 minutes later, a short twiglike man slides into the room. You know it's Barney, because he's still shedding leaves.

"Got what you wanted, boss!" he crows, handing Raven the SOLONIA IS FOR SURPRISES! button.

With a tiny pair of tweezers, Raven carefully lifts the dot off the bottom of the exclamation point. And then with a twist of his hook, he feeds it to a microform reader concealed in his mechanical wrist.

Go on to PAGE 61.

You and Barney gather around to watch it list the BRUTE agents in Solonia — with the Minister of Culture at the head of the column.

"Where'd all this come from?" you question.

"Our double agent, Pullet, has been piecing it together for months. But he couldn't blow his cover by contacting us directly. That's why he passed the button to you. If Barney had only known, he could have saved you a trip to the detention farm."

With the evidence in hand, the three of you wake up the king. It takes a while, but finally you convince him that the Minister of Culture is behind the assassination attempt. When the awful truth sinks in, His Majesty jumps out of bed and starts issuing frantic orders. Soon the police have rounded up all the BRUTE agents in Solonia, including Mr. "Ah ha" himself. Because Raven and Barney have to stay undercover, you get all the credit for thwarting BRUTE's plot. You're proclaimed a national hero and entitled to all the privileges thereof, including a lifetime supply of rutabaga and an open invitation to visit Solonia as often as you wish. That's never, of course.

THE END

After a bit more cursing, the guards fall silent. With nothing to do under the straw, you find your eyelids getting heavier and heavier. The next thing you know, one of the soldiers is shaking you awake and pulling you onto your feet.

After pushing you through a barbed-wire gate, he marches you up a steep hill. Before you is what looks like an ordinary farm with barns, silos, and a rambling country house. But then something strange catches your eye. A slot in one of the silos opens and then closes quickly. You can't be sure, but it looked as if there was a missile inside!

LIFE ON THE FARM: After three days, you've managed to discover that none of the other inmates speaks English and that the prisoners do all the dirty work except feeding the pigs.

One day when you're milking the cows — a skill you've recently learned — you find a strange-smelling, mudstained note taped to the bottom of your milking stool.

Bring your flight bag and meet me behind the chicken coops at sunset, it reads.

Is this a trap? If you think so, turn to PAGE 80.

If you decide to meet the mysterious note-sender, go on to PAGE 63.

Luckily, that evening all the guards are busy watching a special screening of *Godzilla Meets the Hulk*. So it's easy to sneak out to the rendezvous. But as you circle the chicken coops, there's no one in sight — just a stray pig. *Someone must have been playing a trick*, you think, turning to leave.

"*Psst . . .*" a mechanical voice hisses.

"Who's there?" you whisper back.

"It's me, dummy," the pig answers, gliding forward and rearing up on his hind legs. "Agent Porky at your service."

Your mouth drops open. "Are, are you really a talking pig?" you stutter.

"I'm not bacon. Actually I'm ACI android number 008.

"Let's get down to business," he orders, settling himself on a bale of hay and crossing his back feet. "I assume you've figured out that this farm is really BRUTE headquarters?"

You gasp.

"Well, have you discovered that the Solonian pin the minister confiscated from your flight bag contains a microdot with a list of all the BRUTE agents in the country?"

You gasp.

"And, of course, the minister is the biggest BRUTE of all; that's why he wanted that list."

Go on to PAGE 64.

You gasp and shake your head.

"Well, just what kind of spy are you?" Porky squeals. "You don't seem to have the intelligence of a wind-up dog."

"But, but, I'm not a spy. I'm a member of the U.S. Junior Track and Field Team."

"Are they using that dumb cover again? You have to recover that microdot before the minister destroys it."

"Me?" you gasp. "Why me?"

"You're even dumber than I thought. I'm just right for this farm assignment, but don't you think I'd be a little conspicuous sneaking around town?"

He's got a point. But should you really trust a talking ham?

If you think you should, turn to PAGE 75.

If you think Porky's full of bologna, turn to PAGE 68.

The message reads, "Talk to Fortune-teller."

"Where do you think she is?" Dale whispers.

You shake your head. "Let's circle the camp and see if we can figure it out."

In the dim moonlight, you tiptoe around the caravans and tents, looking for clues. Finally you come to a sign with a picture of a palm, which reads "MADAME ROSA, PSYCHIC."

Just at that moment, the door of the caravan flies open and a tall, angular figure dressed in a long caftan and a flowered turban pulls you both inside.

"Thank goodness you've arrived . . ." the fortuneteller begins and then gasps. "But I wasn't expecting you! Where is the ACI raiding party?"

"Just trust us," you plead. "BRUTE intercepted your carrier pigeon, and they'll be here any minute."

"We must consult the crystal ball," the gypsy announces in a harsh voice. And even though BRUTE could come busting through the door right now, the three of you sit down around the table as though you had all the time in the world to conduct a seance.

"Would you like to see your future?" the fortuneteller asks.

If yes, turn to PAGE 88.
If not, turn to PAGE 70.

You turn right, and after a short dash down a hall, you find yourself in a huge kitchen where copper pots, bags of onions, and plucked chickens are hanging from the ceiling. A little man in a chef's hat is standing in front of a long table, violently chopping vegetables with a wicked-looking knife. When he looks up, you can tell he's taken in the situation instantly. And his expression tells you he's not on your side. Behind you are the groom and maid with their pistol and sword. In front is the cook with his chopping knife. Maybe we just won't go into any more details — except to say that at the king's banquet later in the evening, everyone wants to know what the cook's secret ingredient is in the pork stew. Yuck!

THE END

You don't know what you've done, but you're not going to stay and find out. Pivoting around, you make a quick dash out the door toward the airplane you just left. Unfortunately, as you sprint across the pavement, a small, metal object that looks like the button Pullet tried to give you falls from your pocket, making a loud clang on the cement.

At the same time, the airport loudspeakers blare out: "We've captured Pullet! But don't let his accomplice escape."

"Get that spy!" someone shouts, pointing in your direction.

"Dead or alive?"

We won't answer that question. We'll just tell you that this is definitely

THE END

You're not going to fall for the hogwash this talking pig is dishing out.

"I'm going back to the farmhouse before you really get me in trouble," you announce.

"Wait!" Porky calls as you turn and stamp away. But you don't want to hear anything more he's got to say.

However, before you clear the chicken coop, five pairs of hands grab you.

"Let go of me, you brutes," you shriek.

"Ah ha! Our prisoner knows about BRUTE. We'll have to follow plan C."

Somehow you know you're not going to like plan C. And the opinion is confirmed when the guards spray the area behind the chicken coops with machine-gun fire.

Next they hand you a black blindfold. As you lift it toward your eyes, you see two words written on the fabric:

THE END

Was sticking around the right thing to do? you wonder, as the two inspectors hustle you off to a little green room.

"Take off your jacket and hand it over," one of them orders.

You're shaking so badly that you get the zipper stuck halfway down. But the inspector is in such a hurry that he decides to search the jacket while you're still trying to get it off. When he reaches into the pocket, you can tell from the triumphant look on his face that he's found what he was looking for.

The only thing you remember stashing in there was a wad of bubble gum. *What could he have found?* you wonder, watching him toss something round and shiny into your flight bag. Then you recall Pullet's souvenir. Could he have planted it in your pocket?

But before you can protest, the guards start pushing you out of the airport.

"Where, where are we going?" you stammer.

"To headquarters," one of the guards grunts, pushing you into a long black limousine. "No more questions."

Headquarters? This makes even less sense than you thought, especially when, a half hour later, the car pulls up in front of a fortresslike building set in a large park.

Turn to PAGE 49.

I'm afraid to find out about the future," you admit. "Couldn't we just concentrate on getting out of this mess in the present?"

"If that's what you want," the fortune-teller agrees. "What would you suggest we do?"

"How about using your crystal ball to contact Raven?" Dale pipes up.

The fortuneteller nods. "Let's begin by clasping hands."

You grab Dale's hand with your left one. But when you reach out with your right, you encounter not a hand — but a hook!

Grinning, the fortuneteller pulls off the flowered turban. "It's me," he chuckles. "That message you intercepted was a trap for the BRUTE agents who are traveling with this gypsy caravan. They'll be here any minute, but they won't find us."

With a flourish, Raven pulls open the curtain at the back of the caravan — revealing the whole second battalion of the Solonian Special Forces. "Go to it, boys," he invites. Then, as you watch in astonishment, he twists the crystal ball and the section of the floor where you, he, and Dale are standing descends below ground level — and keeps going down like an elevator heading for the sub-sub-basement. "Where are we going?" Dale quavers.

Go on to PAGE 71.

"Underground hideout," Raven reassures him. "But don't worry; you won't miss any of the action upstairs." He flips a switch on the wall, and you watch on closed-circuit TV as the BRUTE agents fall into ACI's trap.

"Better than being there," Raven boasts. And as the bullets whiz back and forth on the screen, you have to agree.

THE END

"Take the assassin away," someone commands gruffly. "And show no mercy in getting a confession."

Oh, no! You shudder. What kind of horrible torture do they have in mind? But you find out all too soon.

They strap you in a chair, prop your eyelids open, and make you watch endless reruns of *Happy Days* dubbed into Solonian.

The only word you recognize is the Fonz's "Aaaaaay." But it doesn't matter. 100 hours later, your mind has turned to bubble gum, and you'll admit to anything. With your confession in hand, the authorities arrange a speedy trial and execution.

Luckily, a speedy execution in Solonia means it will happen sometime before you die of old age. So that when a week later the real BRUTE assassination team is captured, you are set free! And to make up for their goof, the Solonian government pays you a million dollars.

THE END

"If BRUTE has intercepted ACI's messages, then Raven's in a heap of trouble and no one knows about it but us," Dale reminds you.

"Listen, we've got to get out of here — wolves or no — and warn them," you urge, trying to keep the fear out of your voice.

The two of you sneak out of camp. In the woods, you stumble over a tape recorder at the end of its reel. Dale rewinds it and pushes the playback button. *"Awoooo,"* it sings.

"So there weren't any wolves after all. It was just a tape!" you exclaim with a mixture of relief and anger at the way those BRUTE agents tricked you.

Now it's more important than ever to find Raven. But where in the world are you going to look?

Just then you happen to glance up and see a white carrier pigeon streak by. Attached to one leg is a shiny metal capsule.

"Follow that bird," Dale whispers.

The two of you stumble through the bushes. But it's impossible to keep up with a bird. You're out of breath and panting when a metal hook reaches out from the underbrush and snags your shoulder.

"Gotcha," Raven rasps, spinning you around. "What are the two of you doing out here?" he questions urgently.

Go on to PAGE 74.

"Thank goodness we found you, sir," Dale blurts out. "We've just escaped from the BRUTE agents. They've intercepted the ACI messages, and they know how to break the code. Shouldn't we get a medal or something for our good work?"

The expression on Raven's face isn't what you expected. "Sorry, junior spies," he tells you. "But I'm actually a BRUTE counteragent. And I really am going to give you a metal — not a medal — heh, heh."

With that he reaches inside his trench coat and pulls out a pistol.

Bang, bang, bang!

THE END

The *ACI is a pretty sophisticated organization*, you assure yourself. So why shouldn't they use a robot pig for an agent?

"Okay, what do I have to do?" you ask.

Just then you hear the sound of approaching footsteps. Oh no, the movie must have finished early, and BRUTE is on the loose again.

"Quick," Porky instructs, "take this. It's your flight bag."

The footsteps are getting closer.

"Pull the zipper closed, and keep pulling in that direction!" Porky commands. Even though his orders sound strange, following them is your only choice.

There's a hissing noise, and you watch in amazement as the flight bag inflates into a helium balloon.

"Jump aboard," Porky prompts. "I'll hold them off."

As you throw yourself into the gondola, he yells one last instruction: "Pull lever A."

The big red A is clearly marked on the control panel, and you pull the lever underneath. With a mighty *whoosh*, the balloon surges straight up.

Go on to PAGE 76.

Down below you hear the ominous *rat-tat-tat* of machine-gun fire, followed by the smell of roasting pork. If you ever get out of this alive, you'll have to arrange for a posthumous medal for a brave ACI agent who was barbequed in the line of duty.

But right now you've got a more important problem to worry about. How do you fly this crazy craft? You look for an operating manual frantically. But there's nothing to be found in the bottom of the gondola except a parachute, a pile of yellow pencils, some shoelaces, and three dull brass keys. What's more, the balloon seems to have a mind of its own. From the compass on the control panel, it's heading north by northwest. And you sure wish you knew what lay ahead. Should you bail out?

If you think you should bail out, turn to PAGE 82.

If not, turn to PAGE 93.

"Quick, through here," Porky urges, pointing to a section of the fence. When you push on it, the board tilts in. But unfortunately, it's at pig height.

"Hurry!" Porky oinks. There's nothing for you do but drop to all fours and try to squeeze through.

You've almost made it when you hear someone shout, "Don't let the spy get away!"

Porky is already heading at full speed toward the feeding trough. "How can you think of food at a time like this?" you call after him.

But his pace never slows, and when he crashes into the trough, it's pushed aside as if it had been hit by a bulldozer. "Bionic snout," he explains over his shoulder.

Bullets are whizzing past you as you follow Porky into a dark tunnel under the trough. "Run! I'll hold them off with my tail."

Porky aims his tail at the enemy, and begins to fire corkscrew-shaped energy bolts.

You sprint down the tunnel and out the other end into the woods where — much to your surprise — Raven and a detachment of the Solonian Royal Army are waiting.

"We were just about to storm the camp," he tells you. "Good work. Where's Porky?"

Just then you hear an explosion at the other end of the tunnel.

Go on to PAGE 79.

"$50 million up in smoke," Raven gasps. "How will I ever explain this to the Congressional Committee on Military Spending? I'm going to have to take you back to Washington to testify right away."

Before you know it, you're in a military helicopter heading back to Blandsburg. "The Minister of Culture is already in custody," Raven shouts above the noise of the chopper blades.

"Ah ha!" You giggle.

"And the king wants to give you his personal thanks."

You're all set for the honor, but Raven shakes his head. "That will have to wait. First, we must explain about Porky's barbecue to that Congressional committee."

You miss the track and field match. But at least you have the satisfaction of knowing you saved King Idle's life. What's more, your testimony about Porky is so glowing, that Congress votes to spend $100 million to build another one just like him. (Naturally, costs have gone up since they produced model number 1.) Porky goes on to more spy work, but for you this is

THE END

You decide to ignore the note and continue with your chores.

The next day after lunch, you're ordered to clean the guards' recreation room. It's littered with 10,000 Lego pieces, 50 combat action figures and their equipment, and a model car speedway that would put the Indy 500 to shame.

You can't think of anything worse than sorting Lego pieces, until you're ordered to go clean the barn! Behind the pigsty, a weird sound startles you, and you drop the load right on your tennis shoes.

"Psisst . . . oink . . . psisst!"

Before you can shake your shoes off, a small pink snout pokes itself through the slats of the pigsty. "I'm Porky, ACI agent 008. Why didn't you meet me last night?"

Your mouth falls open. Before you can snap it shut, he rushes on. "I'm the product of 10 years of intensive robotic research and 50 million dollars of U.S. taxpayers' money. Wonderful, what American know-how can do, isn't it?"

Go on to PAGE 81.

Without waiting for an answer, he continues, "You and the Solonian king are both in grave danger. You must get out of here and warn him at once."

"What, what are you talking about?" you stammer.

"The Minister of Culture, of course. He's the king's cousin — and also the BRUTE mastermind of the assassination plot. You fool, don't you know this place is really international BRUTE headquarters?"

You gasp. But there's more.

"That SOLONIA IS FOR SURPRISES! button they found in your flight bag is the proof we need to convince the king of what's going on. It's got a microdot with the names of all the BRUTE agents in Solonia. But the minister has his bully boys finding out who leaked the information. And when he does, you'll be expendable, too."

Maybe Porky's right. And what options do you have, anyway?

"Crawl into the pigpen," Porky instructs. His advice sounds crazy. Are his circuits out of whack?

Just then you hear footsteps. It's probably the guard coming to look for you. You have only a split second to decide what to do.

If you crawl into the pigpen, turn to PAGE 78.

If you decide to run for it, turn to PAGE 83.

Quickly you strap the parachute on your back. Even though you've never jumped before, you've watched a lot of James Bond movies. Taking a deep breath, you climb up on the side of the gondola — which throws the craft off balance. Suddenly you're over the edge and falling through the cold night air.

In a panic, you jerk on the rip cord; but, to your horror, it comes off in your hand. Attached is a note from the manufacturer. In the dim moonlight you can barely read the words: *This will teach you to pay your bills, ACI.*

Maybe the emergency cord still works, you pray. But when you pull it, there's only another note. It says

THE END

It's not just the guard coming around the corner. It's the ugly little man from the hay cart (the one you called Rumpelstiltskin). He's being chased by the Minister of Culture himself and a platoon of BRUTE agents.

"Ah ha!" the minister shouts.

Before you know it, you, Porky, and Rumple are all in custody.

"Are you the guy who leaked the information?" you ask Rumple.

"Yes. But I forgot to put my own name on the list of agents. When BRUTE decoded it, they figured out I had spilled the beans."

This conversation is necessarily brief, since the three of you are being marched before a firing squad.

The guards line you up against the wall. And for the first time, you hear the minister say something besides "Ah ha." Unfortunately, it's "Ah ready, ah aim, ah

THE END

You're terrified as you realize that you are under BRUTE'S control. You cower in the corner of the dungeon. Just then the door creaks open. Framed in the dim light are a boy and a girl who seem to be about your age. They are dressed in dark gray shorts and light gray tops. Are they members of the Royal Solonian Junior Track and Field Team?

"Geet up," the girl orders in a thick accent. As she steps closer you realize she's quite a bit older than you first thought.

Shakily you obey.

"Verry gooooodd," her companion growls. He sounds like he's 35 if he's a day.

They both must be midgets, you realize.

"Leeet's get down to beesineeess," the male member of the team barks. "What is a mirage?"

"A fake lake," you answer automatically.

Your captors exchange knowing glances. "Leeet's try one more question about water. What happened after the famous little Dutch boy took his finger out of the dike?"

"Uh, they needed a seawall overhaul," you clip out, wondering how you ever came up with that answer.

"That's all we neeeed to know," the pint-size woman crows, shoving a red, white, and blue track suit into your hand. "Come on; we're late for the track and field meet."

Turn to PAGE 85.

Before you know it, you're in a black sedan heading for the Royal Solonian stadium. "You've replaced the discus thrower who was found dead in hees room," the midget explains. "But instead of throwing the discus down the field, you will turn and hurl it directly at the king. Do you understand?"

Unfortunately, you do. You're the one who's going to assassinate the king, and there's nothing you can do about it.

All too quickly you're on the field clutching that deadly disk, as the king smiles blandly in the reviewing stands.

Swinging into your warm-up, you wonder if there's any way to resist the drug BRUTE gave you. Maybe there is a slim chance. With every ounce of determination you possess, you come down hard on your ankle, twisting it severely. The pain is so great that you can't throw straight. The discus flies across the field, short of its mark.

Just then, Coach Ward runs onto the field. "What are you doing here?" he questions. "We thought BRUTE got you."

Dazed and confused, you shake your head. You know you're going to pass out. But just before you do, you see your score flash across the electronic board at the far end of the stadium. You can't quite read your score. In fact, it looks more like two words. They are

THE END

"Maybe that question is too difficult," the stable hand sneers. "Let's try another."

"Last chance, spy," the woman hisses. "What happens when your horse crashes into the Liberty Bell?"

"You, you get a mustang clang!"

There's a stunned silence in the room. And then the woman rushes toward you. But just before she reaches you, the stable hand pulls a ring in the wall. A trapdoor opens in the floor, and she disappears. *What's going on?* you wonder. And then you remember — the code word "mustang." The groom must be on your side.

"What a performance," he congratulates you. "So clever of you to think of those answers. But we'll talk about that later. We must get you to the track meet now."

In a daze you let him lead you from the dungeon. An hour later, after drinking a gallon of Gatorade, you've amazed your coach and yourself by winning the 500-yard dash. Maybe there was something special in that raspberry-flavored note!

THE END

Following your captors through the door seemed like a good idea at the time. But you didn't count on their hanging around. Just your luck, the groom and the maid are cleaning their weapons over in the corner of the antechamber. She's got a pistol, he's got a sword, and you've suddenly got stomach cramps.

"It's our captive!" the maid shrieks. "The drug must not have worked after all. We've been tricked!"

Suddenly you're thankful that you're a member of a top-rated track team. Even though sprinting isn't your specialty, you know you've got to get out of here fast.

Leaning over and clutching your stomach, you dash for the stairs. But your captors are hot on your tail. You can hear them pounding up the stone steps right behind you. And they have an advantage. They know the castle and you don't.

At the top of the stairs there are two ways to turn. You've only got intuition to go on, so you turn automatically to the right or left — depending on whether you're right- or left-handed.

If you're right-handed, turn to PAGE 66.
If you're left-handed, turn to PAGE 89.
Or make the opposite selection, if you prefer.

You peer into the ball, trying to focus on the blurry image of your future. Then the future starts to take shape and form, and you feel a light-headed floating sensation. It's so peaceful, just drifting without a care in the world. But when you glance around one last time before dozing off, you realize with horror that you're no longer on the outside looking in. You're trapped within the sphere of the crystal ball forever. You've found your future, but you've lost your present.

THE END

You turn left and find a wide flight of stairs carpeted in gray. The footsteps of your pursuers are muffled as they chase you upward. On the next floor is a burly guard.

When he tries to grab you, you duck through his legs, and suddenly, there you are in King Idle's private chamber, where he's conferring with someone.

"Who dares to interrupt me?" the king drones.

"No, wait. It's all right," the king's visitor rasps. It's Raven. And boy, are you glad!

"I was captured, drugged . . ." you begin. But you're interrupted by a scuffle in the hall.

A moment later, the guard comes in with a struggling maid and stable hand, each tucked under one arm. Raven beams at you. "We've been searching for the spies in the king's household. And you've led them right to us."

The king nods his agreement. "You'll be a national hero. And tonight we'll hold a banquet in your honor featuring our national dish — rutabaga stew!"

You and Raven exchange glances. "Mustang?" you whimper.

But he shakes his head. "Sorry. The password only works if you're captured by BRUTE. Nothing's going to get us out of this stew."

THE END

You hear the sound of enthusiastic scribbling outside. Boris must have understood the instructions. A few minutes later he shouts a muffled, "Hurrah!" which is followed by a stern, "Quiet or you'll spoil our surprise for ACI," from his companion.

After their footsteps fade away, you creep out of the tent. Luckily the moon has come up. On the ground you can see three crumpled pieces of paper. One of them must be the ACI message Boris just decoded. But which one is it?

Smoothing out the crinkled sheets, you read each one.

The first says: SUQL SM NGDB RBVBLSY SEQBB

The second says: SEB BLT

The third says: SGJI SM CMQSU-LBSBJJBQ

You'd like to use Boris's code word to unscramble all three messages. But time is of the essence. You've got to pick one.

If you decide to decode message #1 or #2, you'll know what to do next.

If you decide to decode message #3, you'll find what you're looking for on PAGE 65.

This code sounds worse than those word problems in math, you think to yourself. But if Boris could get this thing figured out, so can you. So you grab a yellow pencil from your flight bag and give it a try.

ABCDEFGHIJKLMNOPQRSTUVWXYZ
GOATBCDEFHIJKLMNPQRSUVWXYZ

Taking a look at the bottom line, you can now see that an S in the coded message would really mean a T.

Read PAGE 90.

You catch a glimpse of the old lady just as the elevator doors slam closed. Oh no, she's gotten away. Or has she? You watch the number lights flashing on and off above the door. They stop on 5. Pounding up the stairs as fast as you can, you're ready to collapse when you reach the fifth floor. But you do see the old lady disappear through a door near the end of the hall. It turns out to be the Ladies' Room.

You hesitate at the entrance. If she's a BRUTE agent, opening that door could be very dangerous. But if she did switch bags, you're already in trouble. Should you go in after her?

If you go in, turn to PAGE 26.

If you'd like to play it safe and just go back downstairs, turn to PAGE 22.

Although you don't know where you're going, you figure that the people who programmed this thing knew what they were doing. So you sit back and try to enjoy the ride.

Two hours later, the balloon makes a perfect landing in the middle of a rose garden. When the moon comes out from behind the clouds, you can see an imposing gray stone castle in the background.

From the travel posters at the Solonian airport, you recognize the place. It's King Idle's castle. But just as you're thanking your lucky stars, a detachment of soldiers surrounds you.

"We've been waiting for this assassination attempt!" someone shouts. "Grab the traitor!"

"I've got to see the king," you plead desperately.

Do they let you?

Only if this is a weekday. If it's a weekend, the ACI agent assigned to the palace detachment is off duty.

If today is Saturday or Sunday, turn to PAGE 72.

If today is Monday, Tuesday, Wednesday, Thursday, or Friday, turn to PAGE 60.

Collect All Ten Twistaplot™ Books
And Choose From Over 200 Endings!